Meg and Jack are Moving

Paul Dowling

Houghton Mifflin Company
Boston 1990

For Meg

Copyright © 1989 by Paul Dowling
First American edition 1990
Originally published in Great Britain in 1989 by William Collins Sons & Co. Ltd.

Library of Congress Cataloging-in-Publication Data

Dowling, Paul, 1953-
  Meg and Jack are moving / Paul Dowling. – 1st American ed.
     p.   cm.
  Summary: Meg and Jack experience all the pangs and excitement of
selling their old home and moving to a new one.
  ISBN 0-395-53514-X
  [1. Moving, Household – Fiction.]   I. Title.
PZ7.D755Mc   1990
[E]-dc20
                                                            89-39993
                                                               CIP
                                                                AC

Printed in Belgium by Proost International Book Production

10 9 8 7 6 5 4 3 2 1

Chapter 1
HOUSE FOR SALE

Knock! Knock!

"Someone's come to look at our house!
Someone's come to look at our house!"
shouted Jack.

Jack ran into Meg's bedroom.
"Get up! Get out!
Tidy your room quickly!
Someone's come to look at our house!"

"Quick!" said Mom.
"Hide those panties!
Hang up your hat!
Untangle that kite!
Take down that bat!"

"Why do they want to look
at our house?" asked Meg.
"They want to buy it," said Jack.

Mom opened the front door.
She showed them all around the house.

They looked under carpets, behind
curtains and inside cupboards.
In the front room they looked at
Meg's chair.

Meg sat on it quickly.

In the kitchen they looked at
Meg's bowl.

Meg hid it behind her back.

In the bathroom Meg reached
up and grabbed her duck
before they saw it.

Meg ran into her bedroom.
She tucked Teddy tightly under
her blanket.
"I don't want them to buy Teddy,"
said Meg.

"They won't buy Teddy," explained
Mom. "Teddy and all your things
will come with us to the new house."

Chapter 2
PACKING

"We're going to a new house,"
said Jack. "I've got the
biggest box for all my things."

Pile it in.
Bats and balls.
Games and books.
Jack filled up his big box.

"I'd better get my bike," said Jack.

Mom carefully wrapped up
the best cups.
Meg and Teddy wrapped carrots.

"We'll put everything in boxes,"
said Mom, "with labels."

Dad was in the attic.
"What a lot we've got," he said.

"Are there spiders in our new
house?" asked Jack.

"I'll make a cup of tea," said Mom.
"But where did I put the kettle?"

Dad was trying to find the string.

Jack was helping.

Meg and Jack and Mom and
Dad packed everything.
"Phew!" said Mom.
"What a day!" said Jack.

"Where's Meg?" asked Dad.

Chapter 3
MOVING DAY

"They're here! They're here!
The moving men are here!"
shouted Jack.

"Where are they taking
everything?" asked Meg.
"To the van," said Jack.
"Everything goes in
the van."

"I don't want to go in the van,"
said Meg.

"You don't go in the van,"
explained Mom. "The van takes all
our things to our new house."

"It's too big," said Dad.
"It won't go out the door."

Upside down,
downside up,
front first,
back first,
it still gets stuck.

"Let's try the back door," said Dad.

"This van's brilliant!" said Jack.

Tables, chairs, beds, TV.
Books, carrots, umbrella, boots...

. . . all go in the van.

"Do they know where our new
house is?" asked Meg.
"I hope so," said Dad.

"I wish I were a
van driver,"
said Jack.

"Can I come back and see my friends
one day?" asked Jack.
"Yes," said Mom. "And they can come
and stay with us."
"Great," said Jack.

Chapter 4
THE NEW HOUSE

"We're here!" said Dad.
They helped unload the van and carry
all the things into their new house.

Meg and Teddy unpacked Meg's chair,
bowl, duck and everything.

Jack unpacked all his stuff.

"Let's look in the garden," they said.

Trees for climbing.
Sheds for hiding.
Paths for riding.
Slopes for sliding.

"Neeeeowww!" said Jack.
"Beep Beep!" said Meg.

"Teddy thinks this is the
best new house," said Meg.

"The best in the world," said Jack.